The SECRET of the RING
in the Offering

written by Carol Reinsma
pictures by Jenifer Schneider

S
STANDARD
PUBLISHING
Cincinnati, Ohio

The Standard Publishing Company, Cincinnati, Ohio
A division of Standex International Corporation
© 1993 by The Standard Publishing Company
All rights reserved.
Printed in the United States of America.
00 99 98 97 96 95 94 93   5 4 3 2 1

ISBN 0-7847-0094-X
Cataloging-in-Publication data available

Edited by Diane Stortz
Designed by Coleen Davis

CONTENTS

A Shiny Gold Ring   4

Too Many Rings   18

The Best Thing   36

Chapter 1
A SHINY GOLD RING

The church bell rang

in Wordville.

JJ Uriah took a dollar

out of his bank.

He showed it to

his little brother, Zack.

"See what I have

for the offering,"

he said.

4

"A dollar!" said Zack.

"I wish I had

such an important offering."

"When you are big," said JJ,

"you can give

an important offering."

JJ put his dollar

in an offering envelope.

He licked his red pencil.

He wrote his name

on the envelope.

Then he circled

the word *ring* in *offering*.

The church bell

rang again.

JJ put his red pencil

in his pocket.

He put his notebook

and offering envelope

in his pocket, too.

"Time to go," JJ said to Zack.

"I'll meet you in church

after Sunday school."

JJ told his Sunday school teacher about his dollar.

He told his friend Peter.

He told Angie and Rachel.

"I have a bigger offering

than anyone," he said.

After Sunday school,

JJ sat in church

in the fifth row.

Zack came

and sat beside him.

JJ took his red pencil

and his offering envelope

out of his pocket.

He circled *Sun* in *Sunday*

on his offering envelope.

He circled *ring* again.

The offering plate came
down the fifth row.
Zack passed it to JJ.

JJ put his envelope on top.
But on the bottom
of the offering plate,
JJ saw something round.

It was not a coin.

It was a ring!

A smooth, gold,

shiny ring.

JJ wrote a note to Peter.

Peter, I saw a ring

in the offering.

Meet me downstairs

by the donuts after church.

Sincerely, JJ

JJ turned and gave the note
to Peter.

Zack poked JJ.

"What was the note about?"

he asked.

"I saw a ring in the offering,"

whispered JJ.

"Don't tell anyone."

"I can keep a secret," said Zack.

17

Chapter 2
TOO MANY RINGS

JJ and Zack went downstairs
after church.

Peter was in the donut line.

"Peter knows about the ring,"
said Zack.

"Yes," said JJ.

"I told him in the note."

Peter put a donut on his finger.

"This ring is better

than a gold ring," he said.

"No," said Zack.

"A gold ring is best."

"Not if you

are hungry,"

said Peter.

Peter put his whole donut

in his mouth.

"Oomm, good donut," he said.

"No more fooling around,"
said JJ.

"Zack, bring me a donut.

Peter and I will make a plan."

He pushed his chair close to Peter.

"I think a rich man
dropped the ring
in the offering by mistake.
If we get it back for him,
we might get a *big* reward."

JJ took out his notebook.
"I will write down the names
of rich people," he said.

Rachel came over.

"What are you talking about?"
she asked.

JJ closed his notebook

and sat on it.

"If you have a secret,"

said Rachel,

"I can guess what it is."

"OK, what is it?"

asked JJ.

"I don't have to tell you,"

said Rachel.

Rachel brushed the hair
out of her eyes.

JJ saw something
gold and shiny on her hand.
"A gold ring!" he shouted.
"Where did you get it?"

Rachel turned the ring
around on her finger.
"Someplace special," she said.
Her shoes squeaked
as she disappeared
behind some tall people.

JJ jumped up.

"Follow Rachel!" he called

to Peter and Zack.

They tiptoed

down the hall

with short, slow,

sneaky steps.

They peeked around every corner.

No Rachel.

"She could be hiding

in the bell tower,"

said Peter.

JJ, Peter, and Zack
climbed the winding steps
to the bell tower.

"Boo!" said a loud voice.

JJ jumped.

Peter and Zack fell backward.

"I scared you," said Angie.

JJ put his finger to his lips.

"Shh," he said.

"You will scare her away."

"Who?" asked Angie.

"Rachel," said JJ.

"She has a gold ring.

We think she took it

from the offering.

"It probably cost a lot of money,"

said Zack.

Angie turned a ring

on her finger.

"Does it look like mine?"

she asked.

"That is it!" said JJ.

"That is the same ring."

"Or maybe it is a look-alike,"

said Angie.

"Peter has one, too.

We got them from a cereal box."

JJ turned to Peter.

But Peter was gone,

and so was Zack.

JJ and Angie looked over
the side of the bell tower.
Far below they could see Peter.
Zack was following him.

"I am going to find Rachel,"

said Angie.

"I will ask her about her ring."

Angie left.

JJ was alone in the bell tower.

Chapter 3
THE BEST THING

JJ stayed in the bell tower to think.

Then he heard a shoe squeak.

He turned around.

Rachel stood there,

holding out her ring.

"My dad gave it to me," she said.

"He found it when he counted

the offering money.

He said I could have it

unless someone claimed it."

"The ring is not mine,"

JJ told Rachel.

"It is not even real gold.

You may keep it."

Rachel put the ring

back on her finger

and ran away.

JJ sat and thought. He wrote
offering in his notebook.
Then he had an idea.

He ran to Peter's house.

JJ knocked on Peter's door.

Peter opened the door,

but only a crack.

"Angie said you had

a gold ring," said JJ.

"Was it the one I saw

in the offering?"

Peter took his cap off.

"How could I put the ring

in the offering?" he said.

"You saw it before I did.

I was sitting behind you."

JJ looked around the door.

"Is Zack here?" he asked.

Peter nodded.

JJ pushed the door open.

"I'm coming in," he said.

"I want to see Zack."

Zack was wiping away a tear

when he saw JJ.

"JJ!" said Zack.

"The ring was not *real* gold."

"Zack wanted to trade

his baseball cards

for my ring," said Peter.

"I just gave him what he wanted."

Peter handed the cards to Zack.

"You can have them back,"

he said.

"Why did you trade your cards

for the ring?" JJ asked Zack.

"I wanted a ring

to put in the offering," said Zack.

"You circled the word *ring*

on your offering envelope.

I thought a ring was special.

I wanted to give the best thing."

"You did give the best thing,"
said JJ.

He took out his red pencil
and his notebook.

He circled *offer* in *offering*.

"I get it!" said Zack.

"*Offer* is the important part."

"Right," said JJ.

"Not *ring* or even *off*,
like in *show-off*.

Showing everyone my dollar
made me a show-off."

JJ and Zack walked home together.

JJ got two new offering envelopes.

He gave one to Zack.

"From now on I will keep

my offering a secret

inside this envelope," said JJ.

"Then you won't be

a show-off," said Zack.

"Right," said JJ.

"I will have a *real* offering."